Color Your Own
MARY CASSATT
MASTERPIECES

Rendered by
Marty Noble

DOVER PUBLICATIONS, INC.
Mineola, New York

NOTE

Mary Cassatt was born into an affluent family in Allegheny City, Pennsylvania, in 1844, and spent a large part of her childhood in France and Germany. It was on one such European trip that the young Cassatt resolved to become an artist. A great admirer of the works of Diego Velázquez and Peter Paul Rubens, she attended the Pennsylvania Academy of Fine Arts, and set aside time to study the old masters on her own.

Her paintings soon drew the attention of French artist Edgar Degas. The two became close friends, and Degas invited her to exhibit with the French Impressionists. Cassatt was the only American to be offered such an honor, which she fully reciprocated by helping to promote Impressionism in America. In 1893 she gave her first independent exhibition in the Gallery of Durand-Ruel in Paris. She was also among a group of women artists commissioned to decorate the Woman's Building for the Chicago Exposition that same year. Sadly, her artwork there was presumably destroyed when the exposition ended.

In the late 1880s, Cassatt abandoned the Impressionist brushwork style to concentrate on solid form and design. Influenced by a Japanese print exhibition she attended with Degas at the École des Beaux-Arts in 1890, Cassatt produced a series of ten color prints executed in mixed media. These prints—utilizing drypoint, aquatint, and etching techniques—were the result of her careful study of Japanese woodblocks, and experimentation with flattened forms and nontraditional points of view. After seeing one of her color aquatints in 1891, the awestruck Degas is credited with saying, "I will not admit a woman can draw like that." Indeed, even during her own lifetime, Cassatt was considered to be America's greatest woman artist. In the early 1900s, Cassatt's eyesight grew progressively worse until she was nearly blind, and by 1914, she was forced to give up painting altogether. She died in 1926.

Cassatt, best known for her tender portrayals of mothers gently cradling their children, was never actually a parent herself. These loving, maternal scenes—a favored subject matter of Cassatt's—often depicted ordinary yet precious events in the lives of a mother and child, including bathing, playing, and cuddling. Also memorable in her paintings are various portraits of her parents, her sister Lydia, and her numerous nieces and nephews. These familial themes brought her much fame, and were a compelling subject that she would return to again and again.

The thirty Cassatt paintings in this book, rendered by artist Marty Noble, are all shown in full color on the inside front and back covers. Use this color scheme as a guide to create your own adaptation of a Cassatt masterpiece, or change the colors and observe how this affects the painting. Captions identify the title of the work, date of composition, and the medium employed.

Bibliographical Note

Color Your Own Mary Cassatt Masterpieces is a new work, first published by Dover Publications, Inc., in 2000.

DOVER *Pictorial Archive* SERIES

International Standard Book Number: 0-486-41040-4

Manufactured in the United States of America
Dover Publications, Inc., 31 East 2nd Street, Mineola, N.Y. 11501

1. **The Bath.** 1891–92. Oil on canvas.

2. **Young Mother Sewing.** c. 1900. Oil on canvas.

3. **Mother's Kiss.** 1891. Color print with drypoint and aquatint.

4. **In the Omnibus.** 1891. Color print with drypoint and aquatint.

5. **Maternal Caress** (sixth state). c. 1891. Drypoint and soft-ground etching.

6. **Gathering Fruit.** c. 1893. Color print with drypoint and aquatint.

7. **The Letter.** 1890–91. Color drypoint and aquatint.

8. **Afternoon Tea Party.** c. 1891. Color print with drypoint, soft-ground, and aquatint.

9. **The Fitting.** 1891. Color print with drypoint, soft-ground, and aquatint.

10. **Woman Bathing.** 1890–91. Color drypoint and aquatint.

11. **The Lamp.** 1891. Color print with drypoint, soft-ground, and aquatint.

12. Children Playing on the Beach. 1884. Oil on canvas.

13. **Baby Reaching for an Apple.** 1893. Oil on canvas.

14. **The Family.** c. 1892. Oil on canvas.

15. **Young Girl in Large Hat.** 1901. Oil on canvas.

16. **Simone and Her Mother in the Garden.** 1904. Oil on canvas.

17. **Madame A. F. Aude and Her Two Daughters.** 1899. Pastel on paper.

18. **Family Group Reading.** c. 1901. Oil on canvas.

19. **Breakfast in Bed.** 1897. Oil on canvas.

20. **Cup of Tea.** 1880. Oil on canvas.

21. **The Boating Party.** 1893–94. Oil on canvas.

22. **Children Playing with a Cat.** 1908. Oil on canvas.

23. **Woman and Child Driving.** 1879. Oil on canvas.

24. **Emmie and Her Child.** 1889. Oil on canvas.

25. Reading "Le Figaro". c. 1877–78. Oil on canvas.

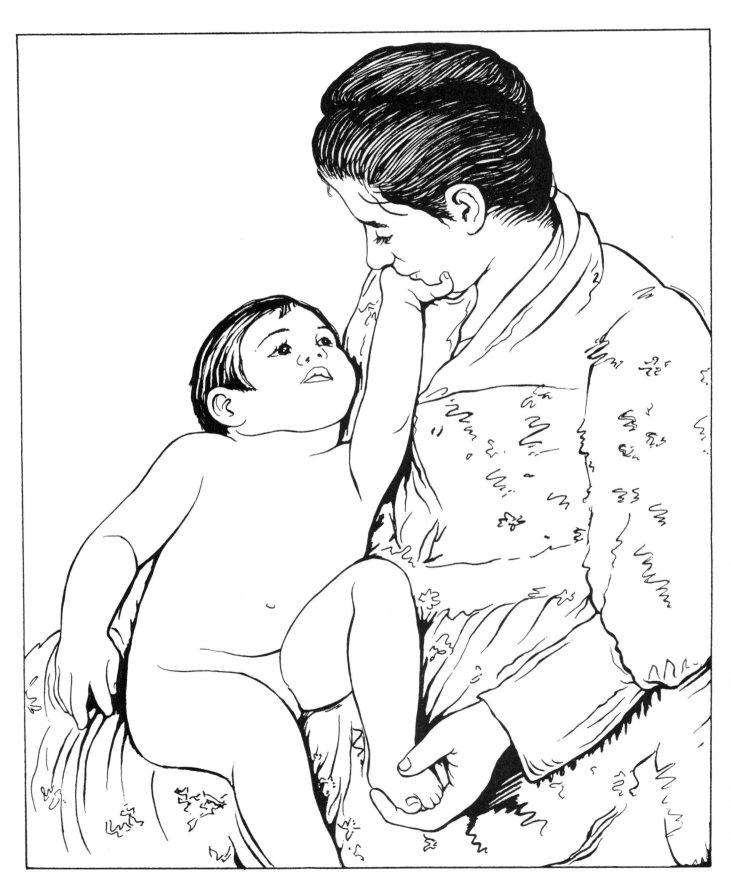

26. **Baby's First Caress.** 1891. Pastel on paper.

27. **Young Women Picking Fruit.** 1891. Oil on canvas.

28. **Lady at the Tea Table.** 1883. Oil on canvas.

29. **Baby on His Mother's Arm.** 1889. Pastel on paper.

30. **Susan on a Balcony Holding a Dog.** c. 1883. Oil on canvas.